Carina Felina

Carmen Agra Deedy & Henry Cole

SCHOLASTIC PRESS
NEW YORK

The trouble started

when Pepe the parrot

fell in love with . . .

. . . a cat!

Certain that the way to her cattish heart was through her stomach,
Pepe invited her to his house for dinner.
He baked 100 Cuban crackers.
He brewed a pot of coffee.
He dabbed cologne under his beak.

Heart aflutter, he waited for his beloved to arrive.

"PROOOOOWWWW!"

It happened so swiftly, that a dumbfounded Pepe could only watch in horror.
His guest catapulted herself through the window and onto the table,
where she devoured 99 of those 100 crackers.

"Only one left for me?" Pepe squawked.

"Who do you think you are? Well? Cat got your tongue?"

The cat shoved the last cracker into her
mouth and sputtered:
"Flummpf flmmpf fliffmmmph?"

"Why, I'm Carina Felina!
I do what I like and
I eat what I wish.
Step out of my way,
or be my next dish!"

The indignant parrot refused to budge.
"I'm not afraid of you!"

*"**Not yet**,"* said the cat.

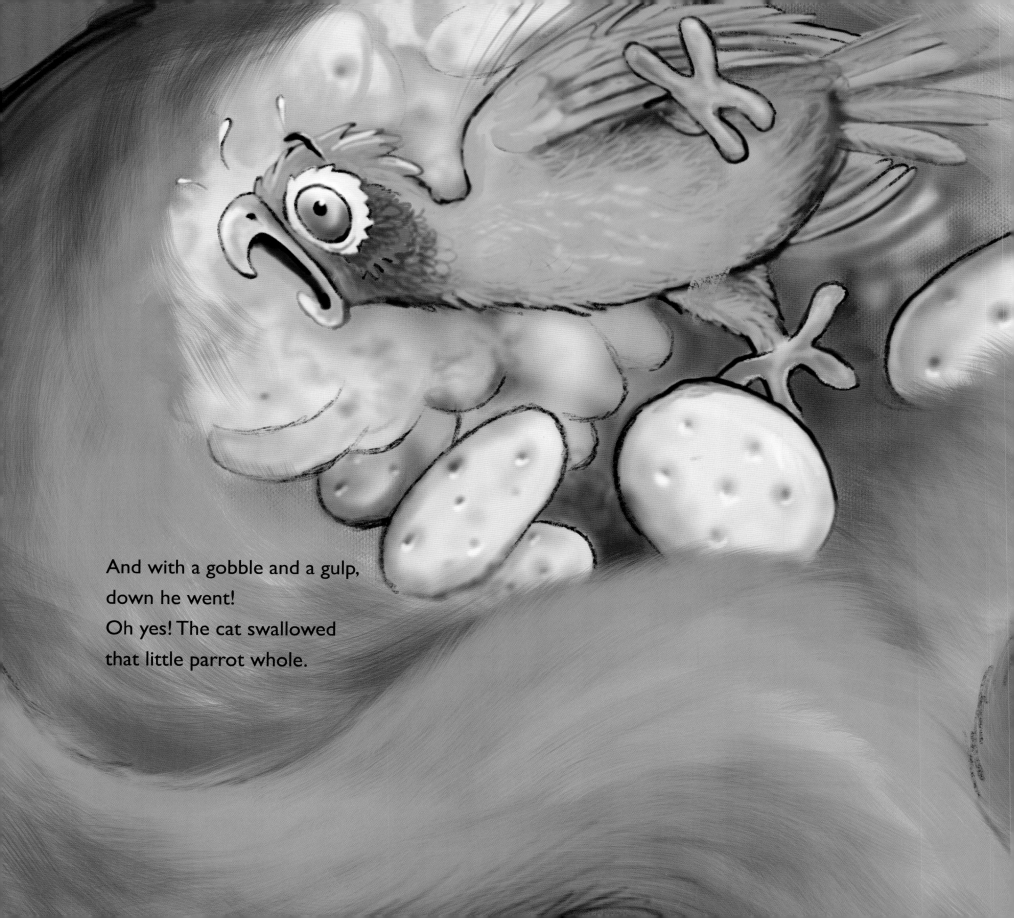

And with a gobble and a gulp,
down he went!
Oh yes! The cat swallowed
that little parrot whole.

Pepe slid down, down, down Carina's gullet
and into her belly, where he landed in
a heap of soggy crackers.

Feeling quite full of herself,
and the parrot,
Carina skipped out to the market square.
As she passed a *florista*, a flower seller,
she bit the heads off of two of the woman's prize lilies.

The woman leapt to her feet and barked,
"Who do you think you are?"

"I'm Carina Felina!
I do what I like,
I eat what I wish.
Step out of my way,
or be my next dish!"

"I'm not afraid of you!" the *florista* said
with a snort.

"*Not yet,*" said the cat.

And with a gobble and a gulp,
down went the *florista* and her flowers, to join
Pepe the parrot, who started it all
when he fell in love with a cat.

The *carretero*, the oxcart man,
looked on in disbelief.
"Who do you think you are?" he thundered.
The cat flicked her tail at him and sang:

"I'm Carina Felina.
I do what I like,
I eat what I wish.
Step out of my way,
or be my next dish!"

"We're not afraid of you!" taunted the man.

"*Not yet,*" said the cat.

And with a gobble and a gulp,
down went the *carretero*
and his ox, to join:
the *florista* and her flowers,
and Pepe the parrot, who started it all
when he fell in love with a cat!

"Who are you?" piped a young voice.

Carina Felina eyed the boy
and his *chivo*, his goat,
with amusement.

"I'm Carina Felina.
I do what I like,
I eat what I wish.
Step out of my way,
or be my next dish!"

"Na-a-a-a!"
protested the goat.

The boy tried to sound
as brave as his friend:
"We're not afraid of you,"
he squeaked.

"Not yet," said the cat.

And with a gobble and a gulp,
down went the *chivo* and his boy, to join:
the *carretero* and his ox,
the *florista* and her flowers,
and Pepe the parrot, who started it all
when he fell in love with a cat!

¡DIN! ¡DAN! ¡DIN!

Bells pealed as the happy *novios*, the newlyweds, stepped onto the plaza. A celebration of guests followed.

But all laughter stopped when they saw *You Know Who*.
"What is *THAT*?" croaked the groom.

"I'm Carina Felina!
I do what I like,
I eat what I wish.
Step out of my way,
or be my next dish!"

"Watch your CAT-titude!"
huffed the bride.
"We're not afraid of YOU!"

"Not yet," said the cat.

And with a gobble and a gulp,
down went the *novios* and
the wedding party, to join:

the *chivo* and his boy,
the *carretero* and his ox,
the *florista* and her flowers,
and Pepe the parrot, who started it all
when he fell in love with a cat!

After that big family dinner, Carina took a catnap.

Nearby, two *cangrejos*, land crabs, watched her with curiosity.

They had followed her closely that day.

And they did not like what they had seen.

No, they did not like it one crabby bit.

"I believe this greedy cat has gone too far!" hissed the smaller of the two.

"*Too far!*" echoed his brother.
"Are you thinking what I'm thinking?"

The smaller one was already at Carina's side.

"*Señorita,* Miss, my brother and I insist that you stop eating our friends . . ."

"**Or else?**" purred Carina, in a dangerously sweet tone.

"Or else — er — we shall take steps," said his brother.

"**I'm not afraid of you,**" chortled Carina.

"*Not yet,*" they chimed.

But — faster than it takes to tell it . . .

SNAP!

With a gobble and a gulp, down they went!

Just as they had planned.

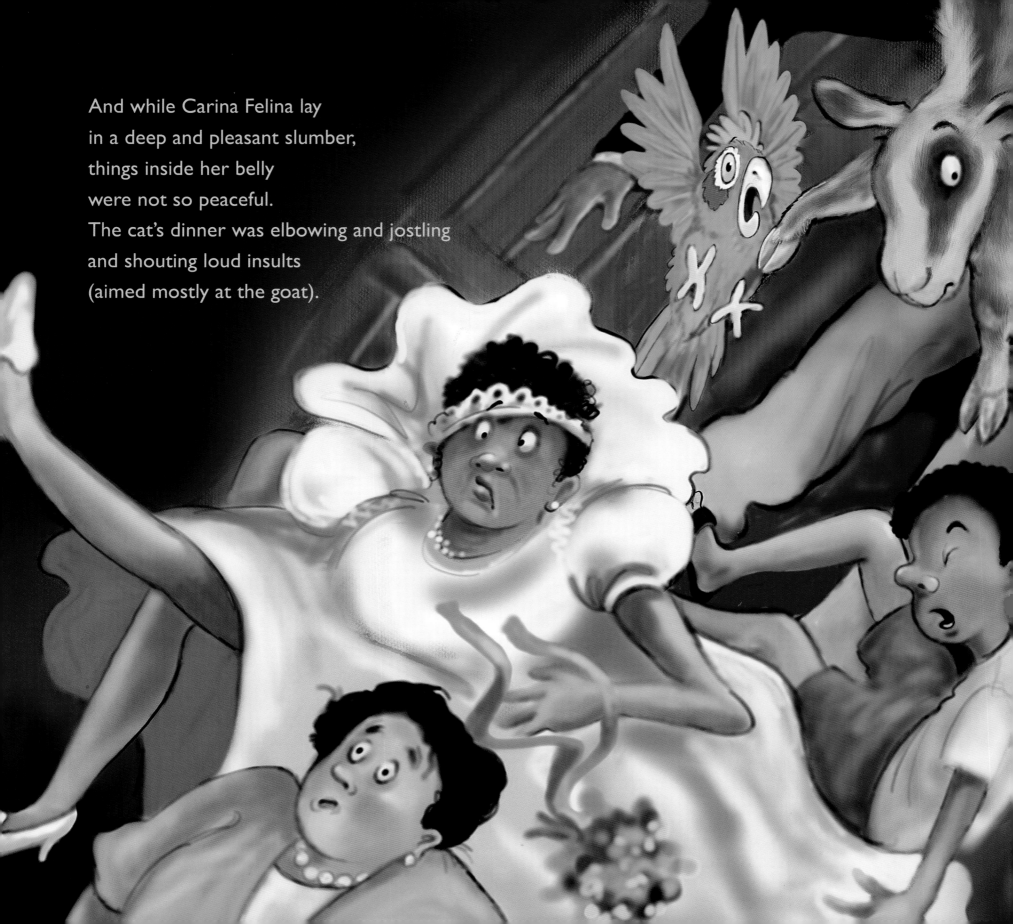

And while Carina Felina lay
in a deep and pleasant slumber,
things inside her belly
were not so peaceful.
The cat's dinner was elbowing and jostling
and shouting loud insults
(aimed mostly at the goat).

"¡Basta! Enough!"

ordered the little crabs.

¡SNIP! ¡SNIP! ¡SNIP!

The clever pair
made a little hole
in the sleeping cat's coat!
Quickly and quietly, out came . . .

The *cangrejo* and his brother,
the *novios* and their guests,
the *chivo* and his boy,
the *carretero* and his ox,
the *florista* and her flowers,

and Pepe the parrot,
who never, *EVER* again
fell in love with a cat!

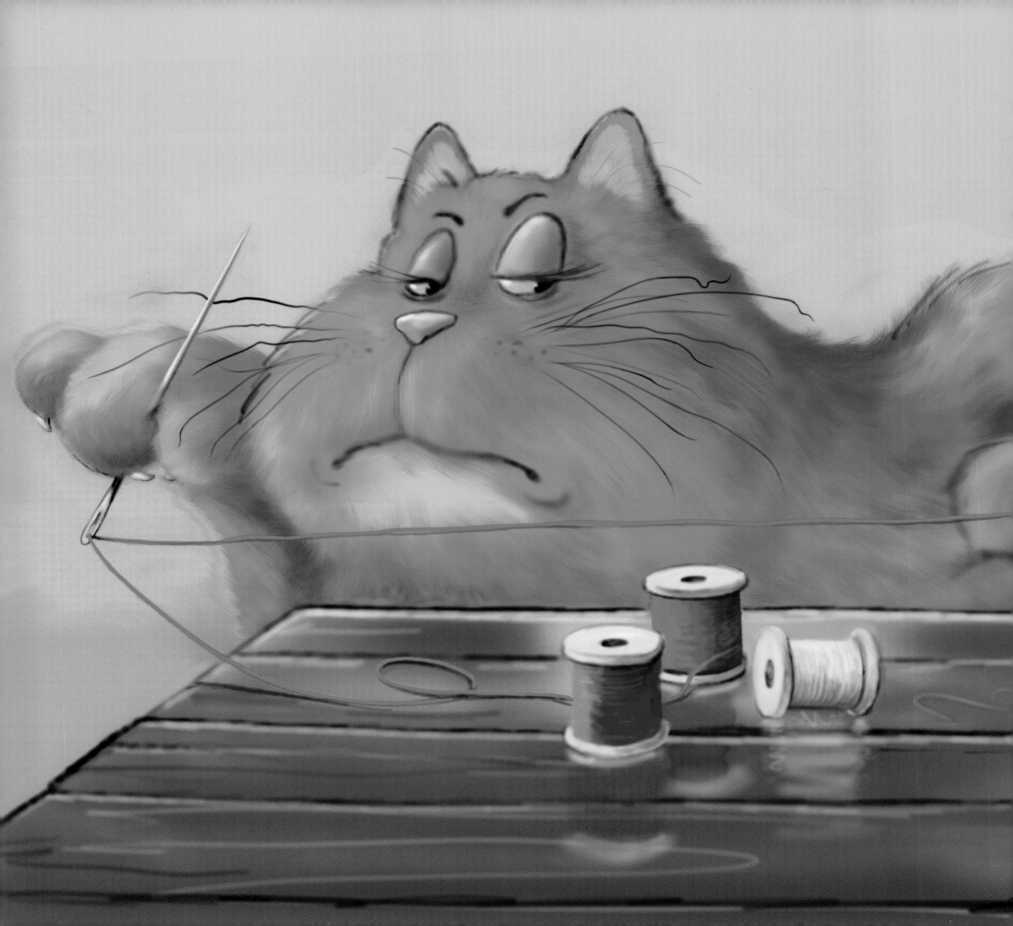

Oh! You want to know
what happened to Carina Felina.
Well, after spending the day sewing up
the hole in her coat, she became a

Very. Picky. Eater.

Where Did *Carina Felina* Come From?

This story is a Caribbean retelling of "The Cat and the Parrot," from the *Anthology of Children's Literature* by Edna Johnson, Evelyn R. Sickels, and Frances Clark Sayers (Houghton Mifflin, Third Edition, 1940), which cites the folklore of India as its origin.

There are many versions of this delightful tale (especially so because everything is *all right in the end* — even for the rude and greedy villain). Not every variant has a cat. "Kuratko the Terrible" has an ungrateful chicken as the antagonist; it's still told in the Czech Republic. Other variants may be found in Denmark, Sweden, and Norway.

I remember hearing a funny version of this story as a child. I found the first source many years ago and have told it ever since, as it's proven to be a favorite of children.

Spanish Words from the Story

Galletas	(ga-YEH-tahs)	Crackers
Florista	(floor-EES-tah)	Florist (feminine)
Carretero	(ca-reh-TEH-row)	Oxcart Man (masculine)
Chivo	(CHEE-voh)	Goat
Novia	(NO-vee-ah)	Bride
Novio	(NO-vee-oh)	Groom
Cangrejo	(kan-GREH-hoe)	Crab
Señorita	(sen-yore-EE-tah)	Miss
¡Basta!	(BAS-tah)	Enough!
¡Salud!	(sa-LOOD)	Cheers!

Recipe for Pepe's *Galletas Cubanas* (Cuban Crackers)

And make sure you have an adult to help you!

When I was growing up, I ate these crackers a LOT. Cuban crackers were the equivalent of American popcorn. They are very plain and best eaten with a bit of butter, or — and this is the most popular way — with cream cheese and guava jelly. Here is a simple recipe for a snack that is very, very Cubano, or Cuban.

Ingredients:
- 1 cup all-purpose flour
- 3/4 teaspoon salt
- 1 teaspoon instant yeast
- 1/3 cup warm water
- 1 1/2 tablespoons melted butter *Note: The traditional cracker is made with lard.
- Cornmeal, for the baking tray

1. Mix the flour, salt, and yeast in a bowl.
2. Add the warm water and melted butter. Mix with a spoon or fork until it starts to form button-sized bits.
3. Scrape the mixture onto a lightly floured surface and knead. Kneading is fun! It should take about 4 to 5 minutes to get the dough to feel smooth.
4. Make a ball and put it back in the bowl. Cover it with plastic wrap and put it in a warm place. It should double in size, but don't worry too much if it doesn't.
5. Roll the ball out on a nonstick surface. Use your rolling pin to roll it out in all directions until it's a pretty even 1/4 inch thick throughout (close is good enough with these very forgiving little crackers).
6. Use a 2 1/2- to 3-inch cookie cutter (or the lip of an empty, washed, 8-ounce can) and cut out as many crackers as it will yield. (I prefer smaller crackers.)
7. Using a wooden skewer, poke four holes (much like what you would see in a button), in each cracker — before moving them to the baking tray. You can also pierce them with a fork.
8. Line the baking tray with aluminum foil, then overlay with parchment paper.
9. Sprinkle the parchment paper lightly with cornmeal, then place the crackers on top.
10. DON'T BAKE YET! Cover lightly with a clean kitchen towel, and let them rest for about 20 minutes.
11. Preheat oven to 400° F. Bake for 10 to 12 minutes. Make sure you watch them carefully, since oven temperatures may vary. As soon as they begin to look golden, take them out. Cool for a few minutes — and enjoy!

¡Salud!

For Ruby, Sam, Grace, Brady, and Chloe.
And for the courageous young people of
El Movimiento San Isidro. — C.A.D.

To Edniel, with appreciation
and admiration. — H.C.

LIBRARY OF CONGRESS CATALOGING-IN-PUBLICATION DATA LC NUMBER: 2022004018
ISBN 978-1-338-74916-8 • 10 9 8 7 6 5 4 3 2 1   23 24 25 26 27 • Printed in China   38 • First edition, August 2023

Henry Cole's artwork was sketched with pencil on paper, then drawn and colored digitally using the Soft Brush tool in Procreate. • The text type was set in Gill Sans (TT) Regular. • The display type was set in Janda Curlygirl Chunky. • Production was overseen by Richard Gonzalez, Jr. • Manufacturing was supervised by Juliann Guerra. • The book was art directed and designed by Marijka Kostiw and edited by Dianne Hess.